jonis agee

HOUSES

Jonis Agee
8.10.80

MCMLXXVI
TRUCK PRESS

Houses © Jonis Agee 1976

ISBN 0-916562-03-4

Published by **Truck Press**, P.O. Box 86, Carrboro, N.C. 27510
North American Distribution by **Serendipity Books,**
1790 Shattuck Ave., Berkeley, Calif. 94709

HOUSES

The book begins as the poem also:

> This Record is lovingly dedicated to the
> memory of those of our family now in the
> Shadows. . . .

Generation No. 1

1. Maindort Doodes, the first known of the family, born 1617, died
1677. He was a Dutch sea captain who came to Middlesex county,
Va., 1640. He married, about 1639, Mary Johnson, a daughter of
Garritt Johnson. She died Jan. 9, 1687. They had two children:

> to make a fact personal
> make it more   than a mirror
> so both of you   come out   alive

section one

I am moved by
a desire to assemble
the families to present
them with a plan
a logic so to speak
or a chart
of where we have come
and why it is that
I am dying at the end
of it all

to make it clear
once and for all
just what has
been involved

                    a mystery

                    the voices

                    speak

A man i meet in a letter
A sheriff she says
My grandfather

a picture (one of many she sends

"The school board that built the high school —
Daddy served for 20 yrs
Why do they all look so sober?
He had a great sense of humor —
He is the tall one"
                    she writes
                        my mother
                            the mad one

and i stare into
his stare
his eyes
so harsh and strange
his mouth set
        a man not afraid of having his
        picture taken

yes
he is the tall one   (6'4" and very slim

surrounded by
shorter even weaker men —
soft they seem
beside his leanness
but not cruel
no

it is that moral dignity
expects
no more from others
than

a selfmade man   began to work for Mr. Popper at 9 yrs
                    owned the store at 19

his own son
howard (a weak name i think
drunken with unknown sadness
        perhaps a wife is enough
fell one night (laid down

the tracks his father
made the ties
      a business for expanding railroads:
         "he kept many of the hill country people employed
           these people were his firstlove and concern always"
and howard
the first born
         (aunt betty and I the children
           of their mature years
put himself
onto the tracks

some mistake
they always sd to each other

His mother was a neat
woman and Howard was
not thoughtful of her

Generation No. 2

1. Doodes Minor, born 1640; died 1695. He married
   Elizabeth Cocke, daughter of Maurice Cocke. They had
   six children. (See record.)
2. Mary Minor, born 1642. She married Peter Montague,
   son of Peter Montague, the immigrant.

Issue of Doodes Minor and Elizabeth Cocke, six children:
(Take a good look at the name Doodes—it's the last time you'll
see it in this record.)

I am mailing you two books. If these are any help to you good. They are valuable only to me. They are all the pictures I have of my father and of his people. Maybe you can get the feel of the hill country people by looking at them. Anyway, will you please return them as they are all I have with the exception of my mothers graduation from college pictur of my family.

                                        she writes
                                            to her
                                                daughter

        Our ancestors left Charlottesville, Albemarle County, Virginia,
    to come to Missouri. Walker Gilmer Meriwether and his wife came
    first, in 1832—bought a large tract of land—many thousand acres—
    built their home and named it "Aberdeen." [According to family
    history, supplied by several members of thè Meriwether family
    and in conversations with Louisa H. A. Minor, author of "The
    Meriwethers" I am of the opinion that Walker Gilmer Meriwether

the tree   is picking
        at the window
                        (i don't know how long
                            i can hold out
            it has grown here before me
                outside the house

        why does it frighten you   she asked
    a long distance

                    i can't remember
                                you can hear it tearing
                                    at the walls when
                                        the wind blows

                it doesn't matter
            she sd
                    there are the facts

Grandmother Jones (nee Houtz) mother's mother was as I have told you a real manager. Having gone to Kearney State herself getting mother educated and her boys located on their farms seemed to fall easily within her scope. Mother told me she was the neighborhood midwife for no pay just a little help at harvesting time for her own corn and wheat crops. Frankly, I don't know how she did it. Mother was the second from the oldest at the time of her father's death. There were 4 of them. Glenn who was about 10 or eleven mother who was nine,Wesley who was about 6 and Raymond who was 2. She reared them as good farmers. Financed the purchase of their own farms but had the sadness of seeing two of her sons die before she did. Raymond seems to have been the adventerous one. Mother has pictures (tintypes) of him that show a sensitive laughing face and the post cards and letters from him when he homesteaded in Montana are so poignant and lonely sounding that last summer when I was at Mothers and we got the boxes with her memorabelia and went through them I cried. He was not strong and the winters in his cabin unwinterized took its toll. He developed T.B. the great killer next to pnuemonia of that day. He came o Versailles to die. I remember it as a very sad summer. My two girl friends Pearl Ruth Bremer and Mary Grace Spurlock and I used to go sit in the yard of the house Grandmother had rented in town so he could be near the Dr. and wait for Grandmother to come out and talk to us. We were not allowed in as Daddy said it was contagious. Again, those post cards of that young boy and his letters to his mother and sister are really heartbreaking Mother will not let them out of her reach, I kind of think they are a comfort to her. Oh Yes, Mother told that one of their neighbors was an Indian they kept having children much to mother's disgust, on the night she was to leave for college the indian came to get Grandmother just about supper time and mother sat upp all night worrying about whether Grandmother was coming home in time to get her to the train in Versailles. When Grandmother arriveed exhausted and barely in time Mother informed the Indian man there was now a Dr. in the town of Gravois and would he please make arrangements to call him the next time. In halting English the man told her his wife couldn't have a baby unless she was attended by a woman.

the family books
uncover
the strain
of life
on these
men

like howard
i believe
in the right
of destruction
but our deeds
are undone
in the secrecy
of their lives

they will not let us die

NOTE R

Meriwether Lewis(6) was born at "Locust Hill," near Charlottes-
ville, Va., in 1774. At eighteen years of age he relinquished his aca-
demic studies, and engaged in agriculture. Two years after, he acted as
volunteer to suppress the whisky insurrection ("Whisky Rebellion"),
from which situation he was removed to the regular service. From 1801
to 1803, he was the private secretary to President Thomas Jefferson,
when he, with William Clark, went on their celebrated exploring expedition to the Rocky Mountains. Mr. Jefferson, in recommending
him to this duty, gave him a high character, as possessing courage,
inflexible perseverance, intimate knowledge of the Indian character,
fidelity, intelligence, and all those peculiar combinations of qualities
that eminently fitted him for so arduous an undertaking. They were
absent three years, and were highly successful in the accomplishment
of their duties. When shortly after his return, in 1806, he was appointed
Governor of the Territory of Louisiana, and finding it in the heat of
internal dissensions, he, by his moderation, firmness, and impartiality,
brought matters into a systematic train. He died in Tennessee, in 1809,
at the age of 35. The history of his expedition to the Rocky Mountains
and the Pacific, which he wrote, was published from his extensive notes,
in 1814. It was at first thought by many that he committed suicide, but
investigation since then decided that he was murdered by his French
servant, who had stolen his horses, and money, and disappeared, and
never heard more of again. His mother from the first believed he was
murdered by the servant. The Legislature of Tennessee in 1848 erected
a monument to the memory of Meriwether Lewis, in Lewis County,
which county was named for him.

All day the wind blew
   the clouds back and forth
     before the face of the sun

         the horses bowed their heads
         to pull at the new grass

             it rained softly today
             streaking the horses' coats
             but the sun did not shine

         the wind blew
           but the sun didnot shine

                it got colder

All day the big bird was chased
     by little birds
they swung in great circles
    above the fields
         where the horses stood

are you still there she said
  why didn't you call collect
    what are you doing in that place
      why don't you have a phone
        listen, don't be depressed

                the words turn back on themselves
                      tense and coil
                  become the facts
              all we are   the knowing is
                      a picture
                  family portrait
                    snapshot
                      i am

                Yesterday   today
              i am calling you
                friend   too

                Generation No. 3

1. Minor Minor, born 1670, died Dec. 3, 1716; married Elizabeth
   Norman, Aug. 8, 1710.
2. William Minor.
3. Garritt Minor, born April 13, 1679, died Feb. 20, 1720; married
   Diana Vivian, daughter of John Vivian and Margaret Smith. They
   had two children: John Minor and Diana Minor. Diana married
   John Goodloe.
4. John Minor, died infancy.

To continue
about grandfather. He served as a "circuit Rider" a form of ministry that was used in the
back country where churches were scarce. His territory was the Osage river country around
Proctor Missouri. He married and buried and comforted from the church located there. His
formal education I do not know. Mother sees vague about this too but some where in the
background seem to be years at a seminary or its equivalent at St. Louis,Missouri. Wish I
could be more definite. Anyway, he was called to the bed of a woman who was dying in
childbirth, the river was high there had been many days of rain, he was swept off his horse
and downstream, he was finally pulled to shore but his back was broken, he was to remain
paralyzed and bedridden for the rest of his life. My father was 9 years old at the time.
Amanda Emmiline Willson gathered her family together and told them they would have to
help her provide for them. There were four children my father the oldest.

Isn't this silly? I'm sitting here typing this and I know you will be weary of such senile
ramblings by now.

your mother imagines
            the plot to be personal
      reads the world wrong
      commits the crime
      and is locked up
            the play goes on
      she is glad she is safe
                  a prisoner of war
                        in the enemy's hands

Generation No. 3—(cont'd)

5. Peter Minor, died infancy.
6. Elizabeth Minor, married Tobias Mickelbrough.

she stands large
    in your childhood

             (you regret that i named my child
             laura don't you she said
             you think its after her
             your mother

                  i mean
                   but
                it isn't
            i just like the name

    when the child grows older she'll think that—
    what I do — it won't matter why

the pony stood over the body
of the dead horse for 2 hrs
that afternoon the sun
filled the form with heat
he stared into the woods
his back to the house
and he would not let the deadwagon
pass through the road in the pasture

i spoke to mother last nite
she sounded good
you don't remember
what it was like

you were always
the favorite

they never hit you
no
they thought you were so good

you were always a good child

you really disappointed them

they can't talk to me now
they cut me off adrift
they will be relieved when I am dead

Generation No. 4

1. Major John Minor, Jr., married Elizabeth Cosby.
2. William Minor, born 1738, died 1759. No issue.
3. Thomas Minor, born Aug. 5, 1740; married Mary Dabney. They
   had five children. See record below.
4. Mary (Nancy) Minor, born March 7, 1742, died 1818; married
   Joseph Herndon, Aug. 15, 1765. They had nine children. See record
   below.

all these gone too

a crime against the state of their existence
      condemns me to solitude
        i must fill in my face
           with a portrait of facts

the past is dying within me
        trapped   it is suffocating

i find its death in this house
a place i have not been

                i live here among
                    strangers
                who claim my body

                the child asks me
                  to kill her
                afraid of my uncertainty
                for my birthday she gives
        a yellow porcelain bird in a small wooden cage

                the man
                is pursued
                  and pursues
                  the shades
                  he futilely
                  embraces

      at nite we lie together
        a hundred hands stroke
          our bodies
          and we submit
            to the lovemaking

        a distillation of time

My dear Daughter:

I am not able to ride about & visit my relations & intimates, as once I have been, & indeed it is this cool morning that makes me capable so much as to subscribe my name. All my natural powers, both of body & mind, are much weakened, & I have sensible warnings that my remaining days are but few, & as my whole exercise now can only be about past times & future prospects, & warning others from serious experience; I pray God may lead me honestly to improve it. You had an incomparable Mother for parson, every virtue & piety; she went to heaven, & left me Guardian for our dear & excellent children; but when I consider how I have discharged my trust, I cannot put up w^t myself, defrauded my fatherless orphans, & widow condemned a slave to a large family of white & black; in which estate my own have ye least share; whereas I might have got clear of the world, lived a freeman in my daughters family, been a chaplain to keep our fathers religions— practice in her house; & now, taught her little son to read. These omissions now greatly trouble me, day & night; & disquiet my night reflections & make my life uneasy. I know you can forgive me, but will God forgive me; yes, I will trust in him. He is infinite in mercy.

section two

A piano waits
for fingers
to sound it

The woman waits
for a lover
who won't wound her

                    ladies in long dresses
                    walking   casually
                        shopping
                        stopped

                                            a hair
                                        a single hair
                                        in the light
                                            shimmers
                                                is gone

            the boy turned
            and turned again
                a good parody
                she said
                    its not enough
            laughing the gold in her teeth

               seeking
what is sought   is found
    the dish of blue   berries in blue light
        emptied by a spoon
            slowly   no   easily.

            the child cried
            every night in her sleep
                        her mother   her mother
                    was not there
                                being there was not there

lights shadowed
the room

she read slowly each word
her lips moved the sound
out to the room

whispers rose above
beautiful flowers
sucking the light away

pulled her body over
the rose opened
to his lips

the ladies sat down together
placing their purses
each one
under
a
chair
between their legs
crossed at
the ankles

the trees stopped scratching at the house
the springs on the child's bed creaked as she moved in her sleep
the man breathed slowly in and out with dreams
                he would not remember in the morning

and you, my friend
                                could not   would not
                                                                sleep

section three

(Concerning the suicide theory, no historian has ever satisfactorily explained the appearance years later, of the effects of Meriwether Lewis, which were found in a "hock" shop in New Orleans. Historians have blithely accepted the suicide theory, and while there is no incontrovertible evidence to deny it—Lewis was, however, on his way to Washington with his papers about the expedition, and also had many reports which were to be made to the government concerning his stewardship as Governor of the Louisiana Territory. Also he was returning home to Virginia for a visit, and there was every reason against the assumption of suicide. There has been much conflicting evidence offered both for and against—the charge that he was moody has been set out by the "Jefferson" notes on Meriwether Lewis, and it is admitted that he was of an introspective nature. Still, that does not seem to be sufficient in itself to support a theory of suicide—and local gossip at the home where Lewis died gave a great measure of support to the fact that he was killed by his servant. The strongest link in the chain supporting this contention is the fact that the servant did disappear *at that time*—and that years later the *personal effects of Lewis* did turn up in New Orleans.

RECORD OF COL. GARRITT MINOR AND
MARY OVERTON TERRELL
(Eleven Children)

Generation No. 5

1. Patsy Minor, married 1st, Robert Quarles; married 2nd, ...Hall.

the book goes on
relentlessly
it records
us

oh   the wind   the wind
      is blowing

i ask him
"are you a man of feeling
he/ i think of sentiment as my piano-past —
playing for lots of old ladies and old men

The night seems a long time
  you wake over and over
    light shifts in from
      cars the moon and finally dawn

  once you dreamed a figure
  stood beside the bed
  trying to enter your body
      your deathly lover
  waking you see it there
      vaporous shining cool
          in the dark room
    a struggle
    it insists
   you try to scream
       to wake the man
       sleeping next to you
   you cannot even
    turn aside
    or
    refuse
  it glides into you
    horribly
  fits your body
    disappears
      you move at last
      roll over

    sleeping anxious
    know
    you must die

You do not dream of death
  anymore   you say

The man goes away a late afternoon sun
        warms the air
                you kiss in the cool garage
he forgets the day
        at nite you sew
                feel a cool breath on your arm
he does not return that day
        or the next

        All day the moths rest
        do not move
        beside the long light
            but at the same hour each night
                their wings begin again
                to batter against the
                wall around
                    the lamp

                    there is no hesitation
                            you wait and watch
                                the moment
                            then lock the door
                                and climb the stairs

            it is still light outside
            when you put on your gown

                            signal to begin

                the house creaks
                a dog barks far off
                the sun settles
                into premature night

    I find the days very easy, she sd
    staring as the light crossed and recrossed
    her friends hair

Meriwether Lewis was murdered and robbed of his money, watch and valuable papers in 1809 as he was crossing through Tennessee on a trip to Virginia from St. Louis and he is buried there in what is now Lewis County, Tennessee, where a monument was erected in his memory in 1848. He was Governor of the Territory of Louisiana from 1806 until his death. The watch that was stolen when he was murdered was afterwards found in a pawn shop in New Orleans. This watch, his

Your Grandfather Agee remembers him as sheriff. He was 6ft 4 and very slim. Also at this time in his life he became friends with Grandfather Agee's father, William Tecumseh Sherman Agee who was proscuting Attorney for many of the years Daddy was sheriff. He was very casual about his respossibilities. his main source of pride for the 16 years he was sheriff that he only carried his gun when the accompanying officer demanded it on an arrest and that in 16 years he had fired it once at a prowler a woman claimed was around her house and that he missed him and the man was innocent and he was glad he missed him. Actually he was a terrible shot since he had never hunted as a child only workked in the store it must have been a relatively crime free society. I asked my mother about this one time and her classic remark was "Well, usually a few words from Charles stopped them from stealing chickens".

there is a lady
lives in my study

she dresses slowly at 8

The wind blowing the curtain

the ladies
sit twirling their straws
in glasses
beside the pool
they stare out
across
the water
into the light
squint
and drink

the attic is inhabited
    you don't pretend
the child tells you a man
    you listen
        he builds things
        walks around
        shores up some crumbling brick
        is restless
you make the house yours
while he is away

Louisa Apr: 12, 1790

Dear Daughter

    I am now old and good for nothing, and reflect with sorrow on ye ill usage I have given you, my children, & myself, in allowing such a mean rabble to intromete with what providence had so kindly favoured my family with, which if well managed might have made us all as happy as ye world could have done; but thro' folly has forced me to be a slave to oversee & provide for a great family, & all ye idle vagrants who want to trouble us & whom we have no business with. But I cannot help it now.

a note
a strain
heard
refrain
you stay on
he is unsure

the ladies walk
clicking
into the bathhouse
one by one
they are   say

disappointed
    in you

For it was well known that when the women lose
their virtue the buffalo go away. But there
must be nothing unjustly done, for if the people
try to deny a good woman the right to leave one
man for another, the calves come weak or not at all.

Issue of Samuel Overton Minor and Lydia Laurie Lewis,
eleven children:

Generation No. 6

The flies in july
are big and green
stick hard on the horses
sucking drops of blood
drawing others
the horses are uneasy
all day
you lock them away
in the cool dark barn

      summer passes
      ladies in hats
      walk in the heat
      slowly
      speak/linger to look in a window
      continue

the last month is upon you
couples visit you
talk
sweat rolls down the backs of their legs
they rise
and leave
you are alone

      watch yourself write in a mirror
      before the bed   ·
            hear the gate move
              trees hiss
                 it will rain before morning

A face of pain
    she said
    the day hot
        building to rain

a fire
    ambulances
        don't move her

    all day she does nothing
    but watch the ladies
    rising
    sitting
    rising again
            they speak distinctly to her
            advise her impossibly
            their voices
            sound like her mother
            a friend, her lover, the child

        One of the ladies in the family owned a very valuable and
historic painting of James Madison and had it hung behind a door.
An acquaintance asked why she had put such a fine possession in an
inconspicuous place and was answered with complete Meriwether
candor: "Well, you know, my dear, he is not one of the relatives."

it was a large chemical plant
they expected explosions
the fire crusted the night
with excitement color energy
but was not enough
they turned away, went home
he touched her nipple
she silent
              the ladies frowned
              and put on their hats
              in the mirror

          Turn your face
                    he murmurs movie style
                         kiss
               she hopes they are asleep

                                   Linda watched
                                   her make love
                                   to a man and
                                   a woman

                         her husband follows them
                         down long country
                         roads in old cars
                         on bicycles
                         hitchhiking
                         in the closet
                                   he sleeps

Anyway, When he was 32 he went to hunt for a cow a man had reported as lost or stolen and stopped at the school house at Gravois Mills, Missouri to ask the teacher and children if they had seen the cow and met my mother who was teaching her first term of school after graduating from Warrensburg Normal College. She was the first College graduate in Morgan County to return and teach actually she was the only woman I ever knew who had been to college until I went to school. They were married and their courtship is hilarious if you can get mother to describe it. She was being courted by Peter McDonough at the same time, it makes an enjoyable story and one you would enjoy I am sure.

a man calls
but i want love
on my own terms
      will not wear wings
      at a midnight
      not chosen by me
strange lips
soft or hard
try to move me
      the voices
      ache out of phones
      'i am drunk
      no i am not
      i want to be free'
i stroke my body
lovingly
with hands
that do not hurt me

      Governor Lewis had from early life been subject to hypocondriac affections. It was a constitutional disposition in all the nearer branches of the family of his name, and was more immediately inherited by him from his father. They had not, however, been so strong as to give uneasiness to his family.

The hungry birds
swooped
into the cut field
dotting it black
their backs
shone
in the sunlight
and nothing could scare them
away that day.

the ladies
buy groceries
at 4 o'clock
and rush home
before dark

An amended note to the first part of your life
which you have not found to your suiting:
alone you found the road
in the country there were three blackbirds probably of
earlier origin as they stared with a familiar glance
at the day   today yesterday   they have been as lucid
as the wind   a typewriter and an indian are involved in
the magic: there are empty chairs and ladies sitting
like question marks neatly folded into the scene
i hear that death song baby
you begin your death lines in slow motion, released they
move slowly like nothing you can think of and there is such
tension in the machine   that it hardly lets go of each
letter: no formulas: the patterns pass away as the fall
did — in one day the sun shone the leaves brightly at nite
you see grey sticks cover the hillside behind the house
Dream: houses, all of your houses, you clean the last one,
unable to secure the balls of dust with the mop
Words: and time will tell who has fell and whose been
left behind

section four

3. Judge Garritt Minor, born Nov. 15, 1815; married 1st, Hettie McClanahan, in 1843. They had five children:

1. Bettie Minor, died young.
2. Ada Marshall Minor, who married her first cousin, Samuel Overton Minor. (See record of Samuel Overton Minor and Ada Minor in this book.)
3. Nannie Erle Minor, born Jan. 4, 1857. After her mother's death, she moved to Versailles, Missouri, where she lived with Judge and Mrs. A. W. Anthony. On March 4, 1875, she married John Haywood Spurlock. Issue, eleven children:

Ann Erle Spurlock, born Jan. 22, 1876. Married J. B. Arnold, May 10, 1914. They have two children: Louis Arnold, born March 20, 1915, and Francis Arnold, born February 2, 1916.

the sleep of the mind
differs greatly
she sd

While he lived with me in Washington, I observed at times sensible depressions of mind, but knowing their constitutional source, I estimated their course by what I had seen in the family. During the western expedition, the constant exertion which that required of all the faculties of body and mind, suspended these distressing affections; but after his establishment at St. Louis in sedentary occupations, they returned upon him with redoubled vigor, and began seriously to alarm his friends. He was in a paroxysm of one of these when his affairs rendered it necessary for him to go to Washington. He proceeded to the Chickasaw bluffs, where he arrived on the 15th of September, 1809, with a view of continuing his journey thence by water. Mr. Neely, agent of the United States with the Chickasaw Indians, arriving there two days later, found him extremely indisposed, and betraying at times some symptoms of a derangement of mind. The rumors of a war with England, and apprehensions that he might lose the papers he was bringing on, among which were the vouchers of his public accounts, and the journals and papers of his western expedition, induced him here to change his mind, and take his course by land through the Chickasaw country. Although he appeared somewhat relieved Mr. Neely kindly determined to accompany and watch over him. Unfortunately, at their encampment, after having passed the Tennessee one day's journey, they lost two horses, which obliged Mr. Neely to halt for their

My sister is a dream suicide
she wakes at dawn
       to clicks
of a hammer
       in an empty chamber
and rises
       to wash her pregnancy
with sad notes about
our brother who
       went to Florida
       leaving both wives behind
              to me
       she sounds regretful
but i see death too —
       bodies stretched
          between tree limbs
          in the woods behind
             our house
                catch my eye
       till i know things gained
       to be lost again
       and cannot trust
       the moment
       with relief
at night i lie awake
listening
       for a heavy step
       a burst of noise
          some thing
                    to fill
             the space
       of time before
                    the last moment

my sister dreams
        of danger from within
like odysseus i see it
    elsewhere

                        John Robert Spurlock, born Oct. 10, 1881, married Linnie Merriott.
                        They have four children: Helen, Deloris, T. L., and Woodrow
                        Spurlock.

        asking the local farmers
if we can expect
            an early winter
        they scan the mountain
                trees
            speaking of
                    animal fur
        and deer tracks
later i see the skins fresh with heads
                        hanging
                from tree limbs
            outside their houses
        so the dogs
            won't get them

I find
confusion
in my families
one turns out
to be another

The Huguenot colony at Manakin Town in Virginia was by
far the largest settlement of those famous exiles in America, and
as their innumerable descendants now abound not only in Virginia but in almost every State, this publication of its church's
vestry book will interest a multitude of readers and supply much
genealogical information hitherto vainly sought.

I am trying
to set the facts
in order

Ere Jamestown was three years old, Frenchmen, presumably
Huguenots, were here, and for a hundred years and more these
noble Christians continued to cross the Atlantic to our hospitable
shore. In 1621 sixty families under Jesse de Forest asked leave
to come to Virginia, but were diverted by the Dutch to their
colony of Manhattan and founded New York. In 1630 Baron
de Sancé seated a colony on the lower James. Thereafter, as
persecution increased in France and 'twas known how Huguenots
prospered in Virginia and were welcomed there, the movement
culminated in the coming of eight hundred for Manakin Town.
Many others came, sometimes singly, sometimes a family
or two, or a little band of relatives and friends, and located
where they would in lower Virginia. In a single year, 1687,
the Huguenot Relief Committee in London aided six hundred
to Virginia, of whom, doubtless, some responding to the liberal
offers of William Fitzhugh, of Bedford, settled on his lands on
Occoquon creek, and some in Stafford and Spotsylvania. In
1700 came the largest party yet, bound for Manakin Town under

to clear the record
as they say
those ladies
of a lifetime

then it began to snow
so by morning
the horses had
ice
packed in their feet
until they could
hardly walk
without sliding
i found pieces of ice
streaking their manes
and legs and
chunks
stuck on the ends
of their tails
they steamed in the
barn air
and snorted the drops
of frozen moisture
from their noses

my grandfather
said it always
happens
that winter it snowed
for three months
straight
we never saw the ground

For the one hundred years after 1750 records of Manakin
are very sacrce. It appears that the congregation dwindled and
in the early nineteenth century became more or less inactive; a
situation in the rural Virginia of that time not unique to
King William Parish.

Emilio came down
after hunting
all day in his
bright red clothes
and told us how
they had gone up
to Camp Choconut
he and some others
and found 7 does
lying together
dead with
nothing stripped
he said   how sick he was
about it and how
it was a slaughter
he wasn't going
to hunt anymore
i asked who
and he   the
guys from new jersey
gun happy
not meat
just killing
drinking alot
then shooting
they didnt even care
i forgot to ask what they
did with them, i mean
did the farmers
skin the deer
     or what
     because he left then

deer run soundless
in the woods
leaping not crashing
invisible noise
a wall between
them and me

The vestry assembled at Monocantown the day and date stated above, Mr. Phillippe, minister, being present.

Ch. wardens: Abraham Soblet, Louis Dutartre. Vestry: Jacob Ammonet, Andre Aubry, Jean Farcy, Jean Fonuielle, Abraham Sallé, Gideon Chambon, Jean Maseres, Timothee Moret, Pierre Massot, Anthoine Trabue.

It was decreed that the levy of the present year be made in accordance with the account given below, amounting to the sum of twenty-nine pounds silver, currency of the country, in such manner as has been arranged by the preceding agreement with the vestry, so that each person pay, following the present division, six shillings and one half-penny, there being ninety-six persons on the list made and delivered to the clerk of the said vestry, who * * * a copy of it to the church wardens.

	£.	s.	p.
—— for Mr. Claude Phillippe, minister, for the present year, from the first of March past to the end of the present December, at thirty pounds per year, - - -	£25	o	o
—— for Mr. Reynaud, clerk, for one year, from the first of January past to the end of the present December, - - -	3	o	o
—— for Mr. Sallé for a register for the vestry and paper, - - -	o	12	o
—— for Mr. Martin for a gallon of wine and transportation, - - -	o	8	o
Ninety-six persons at six shillings half-penny each makes - - -	29	o	o

Clarinda Spurlock, born Feb. 13, 1883, married John Kelly, Oct. 30, 1905. They have no children.

Grover Cleveland Spurlock, born Nov. 10, 1885.

Anthony Wood Spurlock, born Jan. 22, 1887, married Faye Again. They have a child: Betty Jean Spurlock, born Oct., 1925.

Paul Spurlock, born Feb. 2, 1890, married Grace Clifton, June 24, 1915. They have three children: 1. Clifton Spurlock, born June 21, 1916. He is married to Mary Gleason and they have a daughter, Cathy; 2. Mabel Ruth Spurlock, born Jan. 24, 1924, married Ralph Anderson, Jan. 20, 1946; 3. Pauline Spurlock, born Feb. 19, 1927, is married to F. Steinbrueck, and they have one daughter, Paula Steinbrueck.

In the small warm kitchen
i asked old mr. baldwin
when he had moved into
our house and he said along
time ago he had forgot but maybe
1920 or so and his wife sitting in
the corner with her hands folded
in her lap leaned forward and
said yes yes and smiled

he said he had horses up
there then to do the work
not big draft ones just regular
kind and how he'd go down
to get his kids when it
was real cold or the snow
was deep after school

recovery, the Governor proceeded, promising to wait at the house of
the first white inhabitant on his road. He stopped at the house of a
Mr. Grinder, who, not being at home, his wife, alarmed at the symptoms of derangement she discovered, gave him up the house, and
retired to rest herself in an out-house; the Governor's and Neely's
servants lodging in another. About 3 o'clock in the night he did the
deed which plunged his friends into affliction, and deprived his country
of one of her most valued citizens, whose valor and intelligence would
have been now employed in avenging the wrongs of his country, and in
emulating by land the splendid deeds which have honored her arms on
the ocean. It lost, too, to the nation the benefit of receiving from his
own hand the narrative now offered them of his sufferings and successes
in endeavoring to extend for them the boundaries of science, and to
present to their knowledge that vast and fertile country which their
sons are destined to fill with arts, with science, with freedom and
happiness.

    To this melancholy close of life of one whom posterity will
declare not to have lived in vain, I have only to add that all the facts
I have stated, are either known to myself, or communicated by his
family or others, for whose truth I have no hesitation to make myself
responsible. (This biographical account of Lewis was used as a preface
to the "History of the Expedition of Lewis and Clark," published
1814.)

last summer he said
how he had five kids
in that house on the
hill and about 15 cows
he milked twice a day
it was hard work but
he didn't mind much

at the auction hed picked
up a mailbox for 50¢ and sold
it for a dollar he said that
was a profit for the day
in 1920 they hadn't
any heat or electricity
in the house but
just an old wood stove
in the kitchen the holes
are patched up there now
and covered with a plate
the wind keeps blowing it off

1719. List of tithables of King William parish for the present year
1719, taxed at one and one-half bushels of wheat each:

	Tithables.	Bushels of Wheat.
Abraham Salle, Sen.,		
Abraham Salle, Jun.,		
Jacob Salle,		
James Reasider,	9	13½
Wm Gardiner,		
Bob, Aigy, French, Harry,		
Bartelemy Dupuy,		
Pre Dupuy,	3	4½
Jean Pre Dupuy,		

                    and
            he laughed because
            we didn't know how
            to butcher a rooster
            we had & offered to help
            but a dog got it so
            we just plucked it
            put it in the fridge in
            the basement until
            it rotted then threw it out

Second epistle to a dead man:
the rocks gleam whitely in the light
i hold my brain up to examine it and discover that the
typewriter is broken   the indian has left the lay of
the land to the developers   the plant lacking water
grows long and loses its leaves : it becomes clear :

The twist   the turn   the romantic fall
a substitute for experience

section five

What happened
         to
             the ladies:

They packed the bags
stuck sharp pins in their hats
old fashioned veils

touching it with fingers
each one fit perfectly
by a black cloth glove

shoes wrapped in tissue
support hose tucked into
the pocket
close up the bag

a picture postcard
of the local museum
on top.

   Henrietta Josephine Spurlock, born July 7, 1894, married
Eugene Field Agee, May 27, 1916. They have three children:
Eugene Field Agee, Jr., born July 24, 1917, and he married
Lauranel Wilson, June 9, 1938, and they have four children

                              the cancer patient filling
                                 with fluid enters
                                 the sleep unwillingly
                                 it is drugged
                                 affords no
                                   amusement
                                    no terror
                              at first she was thin
                                 and weary
                              but i remember
                              the last days
                              when her skin
                              became soft
                                    new & rubbery
                                 the wrinkles
                                 stretching out
                                 as her cells grew

Today
a day that should not

i think lines:
    and there are desires
    not to have, desires

the coldness of August
a moment after May
and my longing for   summer days
past into sadness

your mother too
begins her dying
another
    you think
i can not

her face
a picture at 18
she sends you to remember her
  before the broken nose
  in a sister's car
  or before anything
  really
  had touched that face
  clean
  and unsmiling
  looking into later
  perhaps
  a madness
  that soon
  playing on the lips
  the lids
  falling to
  deception in
  those beautiful vacant eyes

her face
one i never saw
            why don't you come home
who are these people
i ask
turning the pages
of the album
she sends
            you see
                the voice postures
            i cannot
            come home
            to you

she writes
about Howard

the oldest
but frail

my memories of him:
his clothes ordered
6'8"
unhappy
then divorced
with mother & wife closer
than before
killed by a train
hearing not good
some kind of disability
and it is thought
that he did not hear
the train approaching

his insurance money
put his 3 children
through the university

Got a letter from Mother today and was reminded of another interesting episode in my father's life. Namely, as this month is the anniversary of the episode and Mother always reminds me of it. It was during World War I Daddy was the sheriff and because he was he did not have to go in the Draft. All Peace officers were excempt. Now, Missouri had some very staunch devoted German communities. Those in Morgan County were Stover and Cole Camp. Local patriotism ran high. One morning when Daddy got to his office a delegation of the local citizenry of Versailles met him and told him that the German flag was flying over the city Hall at Stover. They proposed an armed committee from Versailles go over and force them to remove it. Dad thought for a while and told them he would go over and take it down alone. The men assured him he would never live to get it down alone and further more he would never arrive back in Versailles in one piece if he tried it. Dad was admant and refusing to wear his gun took the noon train for Stover. He dismounted from the train calmly walked to the city Hall climbed the steps to the roof took down the Imperial German flag, folded it under his arm and walked to the depot and sat down to wait for the 4 o'clock train for Versailles. He arrived home on schedule met the local vigilantes at the railway station and assured them the incident was closed everybody could go home and forget it.

In later years he took me to that little depot in Stover, I asked him what he had been thinking that long afternoon when he sat there alone in a hostile town. He told me he recited the 23 psalm about 200 times and thought the train would never come. I asked if anyone said anything to him. He said "no" the ticket agent and telegrapher one and the same man simply raised his head as the train pulled in and said "Thanks for coming, Charlie".

I was not alive at the time of this episode but when I was 12 years old John Otten the incumbent Sheriff decided to clean out the Safe in the Sheriff's office. He brought to our house the flag Dad had taken down those years before wrapped in the local paper that was on his desk that day. Daddy had already suffered the first of the strokes that were to end his life and as he sat there on the back porch that day so frail and so ill I will always remember the twinkle in his eyes as he retold the events leading up to this occasion. He laughed so heartily as he recalled that in the next election he carried the Stover precincts almost a hundred per cent. His kindness to those people who had sons and relatives fighting on the other side had been his main concern.

Incidentally, the wounds of war must heal rather quickly as your Aunt Celia was the first woman principal the Stover schools elected. She taught there three years and loved the people very much. Their Parents remembered Daddy.

A FINE OBITUARY

Fulsome and eulogistic obituaries were generally accorded the dead during the middle years of the nineteenth century. Indeed, this practice lasted well into the twentieth century, so it is interesting as well as unusual to find an obituary handled with restraint and truthfulness in the year 1861. Below is an account of the death of Dr. Fontaine Meriwether, which occurred April 30, 1861, at Eolia, Missouri. The account was written by an Episcopal rector, W. N. Irish. It speaks well for the firmness of Doctor Meriwether and for the forthrightness of the rector. "May the souls of the faithful departed rest in peace"!

————

Died, at his late residence, near Prairieville, Pike Co., Mo., April 30, 1861, FONTAINE MERIWETHER, M. D., aged about 70 years, formerly of Albemarle Co., Va.

After many years of suffering and infirmity this venerable physician has been removed from this world of sin and sorrow, to another and a better one. His death was immediately due to a severe accident which happened to him some four months since. His long confinement, aggravated other diseases which he had endured with fortitude for a long time.

The parish at Prairieville has been some time vacant, but as I once had charge of the same, and living but a short distance from it since I resigned, it has been my privilege to give them services as I was able. When I first entered on my duties in that parish the spiritual condition of Dr. Meriwether engaged my earnest attention. He was not a professor of religion and I was fearful that as he had lived, so would he die, resting his hopes of salvation upon a mere *morality*. As a man he was all that could be desired; amiable, moral, of an earnest and affectionate disposition, and he freely gave the benefit of his medical knowledge and experience, which were great, to those who were unable to remunerate him. Until the infirmities of old age prevented him, his skill as a physician placed him in the front of his profession and for miles around the people sought his counsel.

While rector at Prairieville I had many solemn conversations with Dr. Meriwether with regard to his soul's eternal interests, and on each occasion left him, with a load upon my heart, saddened with the thought that as far as he was concerned, I had labored in vain. These conversations gave him confidence in me, and I was urged by himself to make him one more visit during a severe illness some fourteen months since, and even then I was not able to clear his mind, although he was greatly exercised by serious convictions. Recently, however, several persons in that neighborhood, under my past ministry, desiring Baptism and the Lord's Supper; while doing that work I was able to see him once more, when I found to my joy that the Spirit of God had done a good work with him. He was "humble as a little child." His proud heart was subdued by the grace of God. With "due care" I found him sufficiently instructed in the principles of the Christian religion, and after, as I truly believe, he placed his hope on Christ. I administered to him, with others, the Holy Communion.

I have written the above that not only his large circle of friends in Virginia and Missouri may be comforted with the thought that he died an humble Christian, but that the ministers of Christ may persevere in their work, although to their own view, in many cases, *they seem to labor in vain.*   W.N.I.

[Printed May 5, 1861 in Louisiana, Missouri.]

Tell me mother
why ladies
never whistle

Your ladies
are a
moody group
mother
they sit
pouting
over drinks
in cafe paintings
thin lipped
in their
long dresses
they stand
beside
doorways
in Kansas
and Missouri
muscles
hidden in the
layers of cloth
a woman's
skin is too soft
and pale.

section six

again and again
the birds arrive
one day
and the next
is there a day
when they will not be coming
yet this day
they are silent
this day
building for the storm
a rain
to come
in evening
where are the birds
today
all day
i wait for them
they did not wake me this morning
nor did i hear
an arrival
of the birds
at noon
when the horses
stood waiting for hay
now i hear
all other sounds
of my house
the cars on the road
a dog at a distance

my breathing
yet no birds arrive
today   today
this day
of all days
i wait
and have time
to listen
there is nothing
to hear
nothing
to see
of black wings
it is very quiet
this day
of waiting
for rain
the wind
has not moved
a single tree
for hours
and it is april
a month
you cannot
expect much from
not even
this day
of no birds
is to surprise
us

My sister's house is long & narrow & tall

    the ladies
        never stoop
            to climb the stairs

    it is blue and white
      inside
    the correct colors for mourning
      life i told her
        why not

And you are the lady from Monterey,
come seeking a fix
for an indelible
situation

i begin again

exhaling the moment
in my frosted breath
a white cloud
in a black night
& I begin again
to know you
poet king
claims
2 men
a horseman
and a monk
made their way
to the shore
to pebbled shore
waves to be dealt with
ignored
a cowled face
emptied into
armor
its moment of grace
they joined
in the fusion of 2 shadows
with 2 minds
the poet scalpeled
the shape
from it

A fast lay (he claims
it may be a matter of perspective

the light fading

        fading

it was a fast day

        fading

there was no news

just music he sd
there must be music

            the slender man
            states his case
                and retires into
                the ruins
            collapsing on a pile of rubble
            he looks up to continue:

                i say i must go
                & he says that's music

            i am the king
            the poet king
            who dares not twitch
            even in his sleep
            dreams
            of golden lions on golden shores
            in africa
            an old man
                a bitter old man
                    one who drinks too much
                    writes fish stories
            pretends to be for the mob
            but loses that elusive
            quality of   say   feeling
            a 20th century index
            it extends from my left to
                    right hand
            and the whole lower portion
            of my body
            is hopelessly pinioned by
                    feeling

When the spring finally came
it had not been such a long winter
only the cold stayed on
and the farmers worried
because the grass was late
the fields too wet
with the feed getting low

and he left as she knew he would

the man was angry
        lips eyes
she spoke
        maybe get the radio fixed
        then we won't fight in the car
                yes he sd.
outside wires strung
        the words
    house to house
        they passed
a motel a field
    a large blackbird (maybe a crow
            flapped up into the air
                then settled back into
                        the bare tree
its over
she thought

and that was in the morning
        the sun shone
        against the ice
        covering the fields

'in greece we have passions
which burn up our love'

the woman thinks it is always that way
there are no ruins
to shore up
everything is lost
we do not search for it
we are not bad children
gone too far into the woods
our parents do not call us
words do not follow us
pulling us back to safety
at night we fall off the cliffs
again and again

we are not aware
until we hit the morning,
the morning light breaks us
shatters us into pieces
at the bottom of the day
we get up
we get up again
we get up
to piece it   ourself
into pieces
we repair the room
with the light that has broken us
we are not lost no we are not lost
we are broken no we are not that
we cannot discover our malady
it dwells in the light
we cannot see it
at night we know it is the cliff
dreams we fall thru
into morning

how can you speak of love
at a life like this
the light dilutes me into shadows
which one shall you catch
and kiss

no i am not lost
no i am not broken

the dogs
barking
  are barking

  the moon
      full
  of itself

          outside
          coldness
          fits
          the trees
          leaves
          like
          a glove

and you
my love
are restless
tonite

i stay home
i lock into the bed
i drink
the dogs bark all night
          at nothing
        no moon
          no friends
            nothing
              but sounding the silence
            can warm them
                to themselves

* * *

I cannot resist using an inscription that appears on a tombstone in Elmwood Cemetery:

"He awaits the resurrection of the just,
While we sorrow in hope."

                                                            N. H. M.

—here the book/s end
 and i am struggling
 to keep them up to date
 but so many of us dying

you are in
a foreign place
the sun
is warm
the people
seem
shabby
on the street
and
not at all
rushed

JONIS AGEE lives in St. Paul, Minnesota with her daughter Brenda. She grew up in Omaha, Nebraska, B.A. at the University of Iowa, Ph.D. at SUNY-Binghamton. She is presently an Assistant Professor of English at the College of St. Catherine in St. Paul. Her work has appeared in *Truck*, *Bezoar*, and *Sailing the Road Clear*. *Houses* was written in 1971-2; it is her first book.

500 copies published
in January 1976
by Truck Press
Carrboro, North Carolina

The cover stock is Strathmore Beau Brilliant, Tampico Brown; the text stock
is Warren's '66'. The text is set in Baskerville, Univers Light, and Aldine
Roman. Display heads are Algonquin Shaded, Makart, Southern Cross, and
Tiffany.

Designed by David Southern
and David Wilk
.
Display type by Frederick Ryder Company
Chicago, Illinois
.
Composed at Bull City Studios
Durham, North Carolina
.
Printed by Braun-Brumfield, Inc.
Ann Arbor, Michigan

TRUCK BOOKS are distributed by Serendipity Books Distribution.